W9-BXX-861

Kids love reading
Choose Your Own Adventure®!

Watch for these titles coming up in the
Choose Your Own Adventure® series.

Ask your bookseller for books you have missed
or visit us at cyoa.com to learn more.

BEYOND ESCAPE!

BY R. A. MONTGOMERY

ILLUSTRATED BY JASON MILLET
COVER ILLUSTRATED BY SITTISAN SUNDARAVEJ
& KRIANGSAK THONGMOON

CHOOSE YOUR OWN ADVENTURE® CLASSICS
A DIVISION OF

CHOOSECO
WAITSFIELD, VERMONT

Beyond Escape! ©1986 R. A. Montgomery,
Warren, Vermont. All Rights Reserved

Artwork, design, and revised text ©2005 Chooseco LLC,
Waitsfield, Vermont. All Rights Reserved

Illustrated by: Jason Millet
Cover illustrated by: Sittisan Sundaravej & Kriangsak Thongmoon
Book design: Stacey Hood, Big Eyedea Visual Design
Chooseco dragon logos designed by: Suzanne Nugent

For information regarding permission, write to:

CHOOSECO
P.O. Box 46
Waitsfield, Vermont 05673
www.cyoa.com

ISBN 10 1-933390-15-8
ISBN 13 978-1-933390-15-4

Published simultaneously in the United States and Canada

Printed in Canada

0 9 8 7 6 5 4 3 2

To Anson & Ramsey

And to my friend Bill Coffin

BEWARE and WARNING!

This book is different from other books.

You and YOU ALONE are in charge of what happens in this story.

There are dangers, choices, adventures and consequences. YOU must use all of your wits and much of your exceptional intelligence. The wrong decision could end in disaster—even death. But, don't despair. At anytime, YOU can go back and make another choice, alter the path of your story, and change its result.

The year is 2051 and you are the Chief of Operations for all spy activities outside the border of your new nation, Turtalia. Turtalia is located where the states of Colorado, Utah, Wyoming, Oregon, Washington and Montana once existed. Your archenemy, the nation of Dorado, is rumored to have hooked up with guerrillas in the former state of California. So you have sent your two best spies, Matt and Mimla, in for a look. Now Matt and Mim are missing and you must head into the rebel territory to find them yourself. And there are signs Dorado is preparing to strike.

Watch your back and good luck!

You are Chief of Operations for all spy activities outside the borders of Turtalia. Turtalia is a democratic country that was formed in the middle part of the twenty-first century after domestic and foreign wars split up what was then called the United States.

Turtalia is made up of the former mountain states north of Arizona and the northern plains states, extending into Canada. Its capital is Denver. Turtalia is bordered to the south and southeast by the hostile totalitarian state called Dorado, to the west by an untamed land, and to the east by a haphazard jumble of quarrelsome states called Rebellium.

After winning a vicious war, Turtalia had tried to pacify Dorado. But the Doradans broke away soon after their defeat, and they continue to be a source of danger to Turtalia.

Turn to page 2.

You're one of the true Turtalian heroes. During the difficult Doradan Wars, you led a secret mission to Dorado to obtain their invasion plans. You succeeded, and Turtalia foiled the Doradans in their attempted takeover. You wear with pride the gold and silver ribbon, symbol of Turtalia's highest respect and love. Only two others have the right to the ribbon. Neither is alive.

The year is 2051. The Doradans have been strangely quiet for the last two years—a sure sign of trouble, you think.

It's your responsibility to find out what's going on outside Turtalian borders and to prevent any new attacks on your country. Not long ago, you sent two of your best agents, Mimla and Matt, to check on the situation in the untamed land west of Turtalia. The land, once called California, has been the scene of vicious guerrilla-style fighting. It's hard to follow what's going on there.

Initial reports from Matt and Mimla indicated that the Doradans might be working with some of the Californians, planning to use the area to stage a new attack on Turtalia. But your two agents have failed to make their last three radio contacts with Operations Center in Denver. When last heard from, they were some one hundred miles due east of what used to be the city of San Francisco.

Turn to page 6.

"I'm from Turtalia," you explain. "I'm on a mission to rescue two of our people who were last reported in this vicinity."

There's a murmur among the group.

"Quiet! I can't listen and put up with your babbling, too," the leader says to his band. He turns back to you. "How do we know this is true? Can you prove it? None of you people are trust-worthy, anyway."

You think for a moment, and then reply, "I can't prove anything. But let me ask, who are you?"

The man takes a moment to think before he answers, "You've got a lot of spunk, I'll say that. Come with us. We'll figure this out. My name is Sellers. I'm the leader here."

One of the band stays behind to guard the plane—and to search it. Fortunately it's unmarked and carries no military identification.

Turn to page 74.

You try the radio. No one answers.

"Nothing! Absolutely nothing," you say, angry at your failure to contact anyone and worried that you might well have given away your position.

You turn your attention back to flying and realize that you haven't been careful about watching your altimeter and airspeed while you tried the radio. Now, suddenly, you discover that you're below four thousand feet, and your airspeed has dropped almost to stall speed!

The control surfaces begin to flutter and the stick becomes sluggish. You increase power and push the nose forward to pick up speed.

The plane responds well, but you're now zooming between rolling hills in a narrow valley. Ahead of you looms a much larger, higher hill.

Turn to page 41.

You're pondering the problem in Operations Center when there's an urgent knock at your door. A lieutenant rushes in. She's red-faced and worried.

"Haven has escaped, Commander!"

"What?" you shout, jumping to your feet. Haven is a Doradan spy! "When? How?"

"Sometime early this morning. And that's not all! Three top-secret files are missing from our Central Computer Office!"

Before you can fully digest what the lieutenant has said, another officer enters the room. He hands you a computer printout. Your eyes scan the words:

IN TROUBLE—EXTREMELY IMPORTANT
INFORMATION FOR YOU—NO TIME
HURRY IF YOU CAN—WE ARE—

"I think it's from Matt and Mimla," the second officer says.

"I'm sure it is," you say. "'We are'—what? Their last few words got cut off."

Now you've got two urgent crises. Haven, the notorious double agent, has escaped, and Matt and Mimla seem to be in dire trouble. Which do you confront first?

If you decide to go after Haven and the missing top-secret files, turn to page 10.

If you decide to find Matt and Mimla, turn to page 93.

Your helicopter is one of the new generation of high-speed, low-noise craft. The pilot is experienced and talented.

Soon you're at an altitude of two thousand feet, busily scanning the horizon with computer-enhanced binoculars capable of enlarging an image seventy times. They also pick up radiation from living creatures.

You're in constant contact with the forces on the ground led by Captain Ricardo and the ranger lieutenant who had spoken earlier at the meeting.

Suddenly, clouds envelop your helicopter and radio communication is knocked out. The clouds contain a choking, blinding gas. You and your pilot reach for the oxygen equipment, but the pilot slumps forward and stops breathing. A crimson circle appears on his uniform over his heart. He's dead!

If you try to land the helicopter yourself, turn to page 18.

If you decide to bail out, turn to page 86.

"You might as well give up your friends for dead," says another Rebel. "Sellers pushes the limits all the time."

"Can I get to this other camp?" you ask.

"Sure," the Rebel answers. "In fact, we'll take you part of the way. You can join the patrol that's heading out shortly."

You're escorted by a party of four armed people, three women and one man, to a spot where you can see a range of rolling hills beyond an immense stretch of land.

"Sellers is out there," they say, pointing to the hills. "You're on your own now. Good luck."

Two days later, you're stopped by a Rebel guard. He leads you to the man named Sellers inside the camp, which is under heavy attack by Doradans and Corporation troops.

You explain who you are, then demand of Sellers, "So where are they?"

"Where are who?"

"Matt and Mimla," you say impatiently.

Sellers shrugs.

"I was told they were here."

"You were told wrong. And I suggest you get out of here. The fighting's heavy. You'd be better off on your own."

You think about that for a moment. At last you make a decision.

Turn to page 40.

In questioning the lieutenant who reported Haven's escape, you learn that he drugged his guards with herbs he found growing in the prison farm fields. The prison farm is adjacent to Operations Center. How Haven got the top-secret files is anyone's guess, but it seems likely that there are Doradan agents in the Turtalian forces who gave him a hand. That's an unpleasant but real part of the tangled political situation that now exists: spies are everywhere.

Haven's escape occurred several hours ago.

"I'll have to act quickly," you say to yourself. You try your best to push Mimla and Matt out of your mind. They could be in serious danger, but you know you have to handle one thing at a time.

You press the full-emergency warning button that sits on your desk. You have command of a helicopter fleet and a ranger force of highly-trained trackers and climbers. All the people in your command are dedicated, or so you hope.

Turn to page 13.

"Let's see what the day brings, Sellers," you say, yawning and stretching. "It's never good to make a decision when you have an empty stomach and a tired body."

Sellers nods and gives commands to some of his people. Moments later you're given the herb tea he mentioned, a good cup of chamomile tea, and a stew, probably rabbit. It's hot, nourishing, and delicious.

Then you're handed a down sleeping bag patched many times in a crazy-quilt pattern of fabrics. Finally, you lie down inside the tent assigned to you, and stare out through the tent flap. The sky is clear now and dawn is not far off. The soft grass beneath you is a welcome mattress. Outside your tent a woman sits cross-legged with a weapon on her lap. She's your guard, but also your protector.

Turn to page 29.

"If we really are surrounded, then we don't stand a chance in daylight," you say. "The plane is slow on climbout, particularly with three of us aboard. Let's see what we can do about hiding it."

Matt and Mimla agree, but Sellers mutters, "Your funeral. I think you should go while the going's good, but do as you wish."

He gives a series of commands, and several of his people go off to hide the plane.

You, Matt, and Mimla sit and talk. They tell you that the Doradans have formed an alliance with the Corporation and that an air attack on Turtalia from the west is inevitable. Parachute troops will be used. The attack is to be coordinated with an attack on Turtalia from Dorado in the south.

"Even now, Doradan troop planes are arriving here, getting ready for the attack. I'm afraid nothing will stop them," Matt says.

"Let's use the radio," Mimla suggests. "We can contact Operations Center right away."

You shake your head. "We can't risk alerting the Doradans that their plans for a coordinated surprise attack are known. Our communications are too easy to intercept. We'd better concentrate on getting back to Operations Center as fast as possible after dark. We can launch a commando-style raid from there."

Turn to page 94.

"Okay, people, here's the plan," you announce to the five officers who came rushing to your office in response to the emergency bell. "Haven can't have gotten too far. We're surrounded by miles of semi-desert prairie. No vehicles are missing from the motor pool, and no strange aircraft have been reported in the area."

"Commander, how can we be so sure that he's out there?" a lieutenant wearing the sand-colored camouflage uniform of the rangers asks. "Maybe he never left the compound. Has it been searched?"

Another officer jumps in before you can answer. "The compound's been searched from turnip to washcloth. He's not there."

"Well, we'll leave a detail here to assure that, if Haven is hiding, he'll be caught the minute he surfaces. Thank you both." You nod at them and continue, "I'll take the lead helicopter and direct the search of the territory due south from the air. Captain Ricardo, you take the rangers and spread out in a southeasterly direction."

Turn to page 8.

A squad of Doradan troops moves forward cautiously. You, Sellers, and the others who are still alive lay down your weapons.

"You will come with us," the Doradan officer in charge says. "We'll find out what you know and who you are."

You wonder if Matt and Mimla met a similar fate. Maybe they're still alive, and are prisoners of this same group of Doradans. You may even join them soon. Then it will be up to you to plan an escape.

The End

"Yes, by myself," you answer. "I know the President and the Peace Coordinator have ordered me to give up solo missions, but this is different. It's the kind of mission I can do better on my own. The information our agents have uncovered may be vital. The President can reprimand me when I get back."

"If you get back," the lieutenant replies.

"Enough of that kind of talk. I'd better get going."

You feel a tug of fear as you leave the security of your office in Operations Center and head for the airfield. It's been a long time since you've undertaken a solo mission.

At the airfield, you pick up the survival kit prepared for just such occasions. As you stow the kit bag in the sleek, new three-person motor-glider, you feel a thrill of excitement. It's good to be back in action, you think.

Fifteen minutes later, you clear ground control and climb into the blue Turtalian skies. The plane responds well to the controls, and you gain altitude rapidly. Soon you're heading for the northern part of what used to be California. Your airspeed is one hundred and twenty knots. The wind is from the northwest at ten to fifteen miles per hour. You calculate an ETA at eight hours from now.

Turn to page 22.

You move the pilot out of the way and take the controls of the helicopter. It dips and swerves in a half-loop until you stabilize it. You use a combination of rotor speed and emergency jet thrusters to bring it under control. Frantically, you key the mike, hoping radio communication has been restored.

"Come in, Ranger Three. Mayday! Mayday!"

There's no response, not even the usual static crackle. Looking at the control panel, you see that the radio's been destroyed. It must have been hit in the same attack that killed the pilot. But how did it happen? You haven't heard or seen any enemy aircraft.

Just when you think you have the helicopter under control, it pitches and yaws again in a violent swing.

Suddenly you see them! In a tight formation in front of your helicopter are three disklike shapes moving at a slow speed. They have a luminescent quality, as if the sun is shining through them or reflecting onto them from water.

Zam!

A bright light flashes to the port side of the helicopter.

Turn to page 108.

20

Once you've made up your mind, you set yourself for action. Your body tenses, preparing to release its energy in one smooth, swift blow.

Slowly you reach down, pretending your boot lace has come undone. Haven seems unconcerned. You kneel on the sandy ground, fumble with your lace, and prepare for the move to grasp the metal rod. You can hear your own heartbeat.

Turn to page 91.

By flying west, you're chasing the retreating sun. Even so, you lose. Night envelops you and the land. Only on the distant horizon is there an aura of yellow and crimson. Then that too is gone, and clouds play games with the stars. Below you stretch miles of darkened land. Occasionally, flickering lights appear, probably fires at campsites. You're not sure whether the fires are from Rebel bases, Doradan army outposts, or camps of hunters or sheepherders.

Finally you're over the area where Matt and Mimla's last message was broadcast from. To the west you see the blinking lights of yet another campsite. Beyond is San Francisco. An underground network was established several years before in what remains of the city. Maybe someone from the underground can help in your search for Matt and Mimla.

If you think an investigation of the campfires below will lead you to your agents, turn to page 30.

If you decide to try to contact the underground in San Francisco, turn to page 28.

"I caution you to use great care in your strike against the Doradans," Haven continues. "Devastation is an outmoded and useless policy. We can help you to avoid extreme measures by using the technology we have aboard this craft."

Haven looks at Marileva and then at you. "We are able to neutralize without causing damage," he says quietly.

"It would be the answer to our prayers to end this conflict without killing," you say. "But how do you 'neutralize' your enemies?"

Turn to page 114.

"Climb aboard!" you say to Sellers early the next morning, when the two of you have returned to your motor-glider. "Let's just hope you know where we're going.

"I do. Anyway, I've always believed that everyone has the right to fail. If we don't try, there's no chance to succeed. Trust me."

He buckles himself into the plane, and you close the canopy. Moments later you're airborne.

Sellers looks down and smiles. "We were surrounded, you know," he says.

"What? You mean down there?" you reply in horror at the idea that you've just made a takeoff in a valley surrounded by hostile troops who could have easily blown you out of the sky.

"Well, they didn't know they had us surrounded, but they did. Four or five Doradan and Corporation patrols are out there. We've been watching them, waiting for our chance to get out. With luck, we can stay one jump ahead of them."

Sellers stops talking and again looks out at the seemingly peaceful world below.

Turn to page 46.

Behind the man are four armed guards. They watch your every move.

You begin discussions with this man, whose name is Sam Osprey. He's the head of the Corporation. After much talk and bargaining, you succeed in striking a deal! It turns out that all you had to do was offer him more financial help than the Doradans had offered.

"It's a cash and carry business," he says, smiling.

Part of your deal is that a truce with the Rebels be declared. The other part is that Osprey help in stopping the Doradans and their plans to invade Turtalia.

You're not sure how trustworthy Sam Osprey is, but this is the best you can do. It's a good start. Now, if you can find Matt and Mimla, Turtalia's future will look much brighter.

The End

You bend your knees as you hit the ground. The shock is far less than you'd expected.

"These new para-foil chutes are great," you announce, even though no one's around to hear your praise of the new technology.

You key your miniature communicator, standard equipment for all Turtalian forces. You hope it works.

"Red Leader to Ranger Three. Come in," you say, hoping desperately for a reply. "Red Leader. Repeat, Red Leader. Where are you, Ranger Three?"

You look around for some sign of people on the deserted prairie. All communication is dead, just as it was in the helicopter. Not a soul is in sight.

A whining sound interrupts your concentration. Looking up, you see an enormous silvery shape coming your way. It blocks the sun. You're in the shadow of a craft unknown to you. There's no place to hide.

Turn to page 35.

At your present airspeed you'll reach San Francisco in an hour. Turtalian intelligence has given you the name of a man there who may be able to help you trace the actions and movements of Matt and Mimla. He might even guide you to the area where Matt and Mimla transmitted that last message.

There's a slight headwind, but the flying is easy. The campfires below fade from view. Soon you're soaring over the mountains and starting to descend toward San Francisco.

Reports in Turtalia have indicated that San Francisco and its surrounding areas are divided into three hostile segments. A gang of criminals called the Corporation maintains control of the central part of the city, from the docks to the top of Telegraph Hill and out to the Golden Gate Bridge. Or, what once was the Golden Gate Bridge—now it's nothing but jumbled concrete, metal, and cable on either side of the bay, with no bridge spanning water.

The Corporation is a mixture of military people, gamblers, and drug dealers. It's headed by the president of a famous high-tech company. He has turned his creative genius to the organization of political power over a once populous and successful city. There is apparent madness in his appetite for raw power.

Turn to page 42.

Sleep comes quickly, perhaps due to drugs in the tea, perhaps due to the fatigue of a long day. Dreams cascade through your head. At one point you're running wildly up a steep, sloping path, desperate to gain the top—except that the path goes on forever.

Later you dream that you're back in school, taking exams, but you can't remember what subjects you've studied or what exams you must take. You toss and turn, thrashing inside the narrow sleeping bag. Then you dream that you've found Matt and Mimla. This dream seems very real. Only you can't understand why Mimla is shaking you.

Turn to page 89.

You put the motor-glider into a long, slow banking turn. At eight thousand feet it's very difficult to make out the details of the terrain. You kick the rudder pedal and push the stick over and forward. Your plane sideslips quietly and effortlessly until the altimeter reads six thousand feet. There are rolling hills below, and you feel that this is the safest altitude for now. You level off and cut back on the throttle.

Scanning the country around the campsites, you see ample landing room in grassy open spaces. One field is fairly close to one of the campfires.

"I wonder if I should try radio contact," you say to yourself. "It's risky. It'd be a dead giveaway if those are hostile troops. On the other hand, it would save time and be safer if I could get someone to help check the field before I land."

If you try to make radio contact, turn to page 4.

*If you decide to go in without radio contact,
turn to page 37.*

"Okay, Haven, or whoever you are, I'll take a chance and go aboard this thing of yours." Your curiosity is so great that you can't give up this opportunity to board a spacecraft.

"Fine. I thought you'd agree. You are a thoughtful and intelligent creature, Commander," Haven says.

He reaches out again and takes your hand. Seconds later you materialize inside the craft. Nothing about the outside of the silvery craft, with its smooth, metallic skin, prepared you for what you'd find inside. You look around in surprise at the glass-like, many-faceted interior. It's like being inside a diamond.

"Where are we?" you blurt out, stunned by the brilliant, multicolored light that reflects inwardly from the facets.

"We are within a complex carbon atom that has been enlarged to a size appropriate for earth voyaging," replies a creature that has appeared beside Haven. The creature is square, sharp-edged, and metallic gray, with red plastic fittings.

Before your eyes it develops mechanical arms and legs, a body, and a head. It reminds you of something you've read about—the Japanese "Transformer" toys that were so popular years ago in the former United States.

Turn to page 53.

"Look, I'm just an ordinary civilian," you say. "My brother's been living outside of San Francisco for years. He moved there before the bad times. I'm trying to find him. I want . . ."

"Stop right there, " the man with the lamp says. "You look honest. I follow instincts. I don't believe your story, but for some oddball reason, I trust you. I'm called Sellers, and these are—"

Just then an owl hoots. Sellers holds his hand up.

"Quiet!" he whispers to you. "That's one of my people. There could be company we don't need or want around here."

Two shots are fired. They're accurate: two of the civilians near you slump to the ground.

"Hold your fire," Sellers yells to his people. "Every shot must count."

He grabs you by the arm and pulls you down behind a jumble of boulders.

"Here, use this if you want," he says, handing you an automatic weapon. He also hands you two clips of ammunition. "We Rebels don't have much ammunition, so use it wisely."

Turn to page 34.

Gunfire fills the air. You look toward your plane just in time to see a barrage of bullets slam into it. There's a muffled whump as the gas tank explodes. In minutes your plane becomes a twisted, ugly, black tangle of metal and melted plastic.

Sellers grabs your arm again.

"Sorry about all this. You may be better off on your own. I wouldn't blame you if you want to slip away into the woods."

If you decide to slip away on your own, turn to page 38.

If you decide to stay with Sellers, turn to page 40.

A beam of sky-blue light reaches down from the underside of the craft and bathes you in its warm energy. You try to move, to step out of the beam. But your feet are locked in position! You try to raise your arm, but it remains at your side. Your breathing slows, and your pulse rate falls until your heart is beating so slowly that you can feel each pulse in its full rhythmic movement.

In rapid stages Haven materializes beside you: first his head and shoulders, then his whole body. Slowly, facial details and coloration are added. The apparition reaches out and touches you—and the touch releases you from the frozen state you've been in.

Turn to page 45.

You scan your instruments, automatically checking your airspeed and altimeter reading. Landing on an unknown field can be tricky.

"But not as tricky as using the radio when there may be Doradans around," you remind yourself out loud. The crackle of your voice in the dimly lit cabin of the motor-glider sounds unreal to you.

You repeatedly scan the sky for other aircraft and watch the clouds as they pass between you and the land. Twice you circle what seems to be the best landing spot. Then you set up for landing and begin the final approach.

"Flaps down, airspeed correct, wings level," you tell yourself, staring into the fast-approaching dark area of grassy field.

Your plane pitches and rolls in changing air. You move the controls gingerly but knowingly.

Turn to page 51.

"You may be right, Sellers. Goodbye and good luck. I hope you make it," you tell him.

"Yeah, see you around, " he replies, then turns to the job at hand.

You saw where your kit bag was dropped when the shooting started, and you're able to find it in the dark. All around you people are fighting for their lives. You wonder how many others will try to slip away into the night and escape the madness of gunfire.

You shrug into the shoulder straps of the kit bag and crawl back from the ring of fire, moving like a snail, hoping to get away unnoticed.

The intensity of the battle eases, and you rise to a crouching position. You begin to run, bent low over the ground. Nothing happens! You're still alive. You haven't been seen.

You cover a hundred yards, stop, catch your breath, then travel another hundred yards and stop again. Gunfire erupts with renewed ferocity. You now hear the persistent and ominous thump of mortar rounds. Cries of pain and terror are carried through the night air. You keep moving.

Turn to page 92.

Haven and the humanoid fling you from the crystal spaceship. You hit the sandy ground with a grinding thud!

The ship disappears. Moments later you're surrounded by your ranger force. Your memory has begun to fade. You remember nothing about Haven and the ship.

But your memory loss doesn't stop there. Soon you don't even remember who you are, where you're from, or who the people surrounding you are. Within an hour you have lost the ability to speak. All sounds become unintelligible, except for a wailing cry—and the cry is coming from you!

You now have the mind of a three-week-old infant. Haven has taken his revenge.

The End

40

"I'm staying, Sellers," you say. "I'm determined to do what I came to do. Anyway, you need all the help you can get."

"Fine. But remember, it's your neck," he replies.

The fighting is intense. You're too busy defending your life to search for Matt and Mimla. There seems little hope of getting out alive. You think about your life in Turtalia and what the freedom of choice has meant for your people. The firing eases at times, and hope renews at these moments.

"I can't see who we're fighting," you say to Sellers.

"It's always like that," he replies. "Ambushes, hit and run. Actually, we use the same tactics. All the same, it just means killing people."

Soon the firing begins again. It seems impossible that anyone will survive the awful violence.

Suddenly you're out of ammunition!

Turn to page 44.

"Yikes!" you yell as you pull back on the stick, giving the plane full throttle. You barely make it over the crest of the hill.

"That would've been a dumb way to die," you scold yourself. "I've got to get a grip, or else I'll never find Matt and Mimla."

At that moment a heat-seeking rocket rises from one of the campsites below.

The small fireball from your exploding plane is greeted with great joy by the Doradan patrol that launched the rocket.

The End

Intelligence reports also have indicated that factions within the Corporation want the president out—indeed, want him dead. But he seems to have a genius for survival. He's unpredictable, unfair, and brilliant.

The other two groups in and around San Francisco are resistance factions fighting the Corporation. They vie with one another for the support of a dazed, poverty-stricken, and frightened population. One group is called the Rebels; the other changes its name about as often as the weather changes. Your contact is a member of the Rebels.

The airport for which you're heading is in a disputed area. Since your plane can also land in a small field, you decide against trying the airport and instead look for the playing fields on the former University of California campus in Berkeley. The university is closed, of course. What remains of it lies in a San Francisco Bay district reported to be under the control of the Rebels.

Turn to page 48.

44

"Sellers, I'm out," you say. "Have you got any more clips?"

"Nope. That's it, I'm afraid. I ran out minutes ago myself."

Soon all of the Rebels are out of ammunition. The attackers sense what has happened, but they're cautious. They hold their positions, suspecting the Rebels might be bluffing.

Finally, they contact you through a loudspeaker.

"Throw down your arms! There is no alternative. I repeat, stand up and throw down your weapons!"

Sellers nods and shrugs his shoulders. "Let's see what happens."

Turn to page 15.

Haven speaks. "I am certain you did not expect this, did you? I have more power than you imagined." His tone is slow and even. There's no harshness in his voice.

You nod your head. He continues.

"I have never been a Doradan, you know. Actually, I am not human. You can tell by my craft here. I am of a society called the Crystal People. The people of my world need the help of the people of your world. I could not be sure whether the Doradans or you Turtalians should be the ones to help. I have now decided in favor of the people of Turtalia. Will you come aboard my craft and find out what we need? We are friendly."

"What happens if I refuse?" you reply.

"Nothing at all. You are free to go."

"What about my pilot? If you're so friendly, why did you kill him?" you ask.

"It was not us who killed your pilot. Are you sure your own people are reliable?" Haven replies.

At that moment you catch sight of three figures moving toward you in the distance. They're members of the Turtalian ranger force.

If you decide to trust Haven for the time being, turn to page 31.

If you decide to make a dash for freedom and join your own people, turn to page 49.

Blindly you follow the directions Sellers gives you.

"I hope we're getting close," you tell him after you've been flying for some time. "Looks like bad weather ahead."

He nods silently, and you turn your attention back to your flying. Soon the sky is filled with towering thunderheads capable of ripping the wings off any airplane—and especially off the delicate motor-glider you're flying. You dodge in and out of the clouds, climbing, diving, banking, and turning. Lightning flashes all around you, illuminating the clouds as though someone were switching on lamps inside them. The wind currents at twelve thousand feet gust well over forty knots, and your plane is tossed like a toy.

You fly on and on, battling to stay in the air. Twice you slip through the clouds looking for a place to land, but without success.

Turn to page 62.

48

Minutes later you spot the football field and decide from a careful check that it's probably safe to land there. You don't try making radio contact.

The landing is easy. The plane comes to a stop at what used to be the fifty-yard line. No one is about. You climb out of the cockpit, grab your kit bag, and head out to find the man named Jeremy, your Rebel contact.

Turn to page 95.

You drop to the ground, knocking Haven down with a kick to his legs. Before he can respond, you're on your feet and running in the direction of the three rangers.

"Don't fire. It's me!" you shout. But they're too far away to identify you. They watch your approach warily.

You run as hard as you can. There's no looking back. At any moment you expect a shot or a paralyzing ray to hit you. *Haven won't give me up too easily,* you think.

No shot rings out. No paralyzing ray stops you. The rangers stand with weapons at the ready. You make one final burst forward and reach the safety of the group.

"Thank heavens you're here," you gasp. "I've never been so happy—"

You stop when you see their grim faces. You suddenly realize that no one has moved forward to help you.

"Don't move, Commander. You can't escape," says a lieutenant newly assigned to the ranger force. "Don't move or you'll never move again."

"What do you mean?" you cry. "Drop those weapons! Don't you dare aim them at me!"

Turn to page 55.

The wheels of your motor-glider touch the earth. The plane rolls through the grass, bumping across uneven ground. You kick the rudder pedals several times, trying to avoid what looks like rocks or bumps in the terrain. Your efforts don't do much good.

With one last jolt, the plane comes to a stop.

"Not bad," you congratulate yourself as you unlatch the canopy. Cool, fragrant night air rushes over you.

You stretch, then unsnap your seat belt and shoulder harness. Once you flick off the switches, the plane becomes a silent, motionless piece of the landscape.

Your survival kit is in the backseat. You reach around, pick it up, and step out of the cockpit and onto the wing.

Go on to the next page.

The lieutenant motions to one of the others, who snaps handcuffs on your wrists. From behind some scrub pine a squad of soldiers emerges, wearing the uniform of the Doradan army!

"Well done, Lieutenant!" Haven says. He has suddenly appeared at your side. "Leave this Earthling to me."

The ranger lieutenant snaps a salute and turns to talk with the Doradans.

"Where are my troops?" you ask, dreading the answer.

"We've taken care of them, don't worry," replies the turncoat lieutenant.

Haven leads you back toward the spacecraft.

"So, you've won after all, haven't you, Haven?" you say in a disgusted tone.

"Be calm, Commander. Nothing is ever what it appears to be. I am as anxious to be free of these Doradans as you are. They are fascists. Our intelligence has analyzed their system; fascism will not work in the long run. As I told you, we need help, and we want it from you Turtalians. Will you contact your home base and report our position? Your forces can capture the Doradans, and we can begin discussions on how to help one another."

If you use your communicator to contact Operations Center, turn to page 57.

If you decide to fake the communication, turn to page 64.

56

"For some reason I believe you, Haven, despite your past history of having helped the Doradans," you say. "After all, you didn't know how bad the Doradans really are. First, though, tell me more. I need to know all about you."

"It will take time, Commander, unless you will allow me to do a Rapid Information Transfer with our crystal circuit."

"I don't know. My circuits are humanoid; they might not interface with yours," you reply.

"Do not worry," Haven says. "We have analyzed the human construction and will tap in appropriately."

Turn to page 117.

Your call to Operations Center results in an immediate response to your request for help with the Doradans. With little or no firing, a Turtalian strike force rounds up the Doradan team. Your ranger force, being held prisoner two miles from the spacecraft, is quickly located. They'd been immobilized by an old-fashioned gas once used by police to quell protests during the political clashes of the 1960s in the United States. Its effectiveness was temporary, and exposure to the gas caused no residual harm—just tearstained faces.

Aboard the Turtalian command craft is the chief political officer of Turtalia, a woman named Marileva.

"I'm anxious to talk with this being—this Haven—who paraded as the Doradan spy. Where is he?" she asks you.

"Why, right here," you reply. You turn to find that no one is standing beside you. "He was here a minute ago!"

"Have no fear." The voice of Haven floats in the air. "I am just resting for a bit. It is quite fatiguing to be in humanoid form for too long."

Turn to page 61.

"Morning. Nice day," you say as you move toward the counter, hoping nonchalance will break the ice. "Coffee, please."

"No coffee. What do you think we are, a civilized nation, bud? It's herb tea, like it or lump it. That's all we've got. That's all we've had for seven long years."

"Fine. That will do just fine."

You sit huddled over the strong, aromatic tea. Finally, you summon your courage. "You wouldn't happen to have an old copy of *The New York Times* around, would you?" you ask the waiter. It's your code. If the waiter is Jeremy, he'll recognize it.

He looks at you and asks, "What date?"

Turn to page 70.

Haven's body begins to rematerialize beside you.

"I have information important to you Turtalians," he says. "The Doradans plan to launch a surprise attack on your capital in Denver within the next week. I recommend striking their capital first. We can use my forces and my craft. Will you accept our aid?" he asks. "Of course, we want something in return."

If you want to accept, turn to page 65.

If you want to reject his offer of help, turn to page 72.

Time passes in agonizing minutes. Hope for a break in the storm is the only thing that keeps you going. Finally, you enter a cloud so dense and so high that you pray you will get out of it alive.

Your prayer is not answered. You and Sellers and your airplane meet the unyielding rock face of a mountain hidden by the clouds. The end comes mercifully fast.

The End

"Sure, Haven, I'll contact my home base," you say as you fiddle with the communicator, stalling for time. You have a hunch that Haven is trying to invade your security wavelength and head up a Doradan takeover attack.

Haven nods and turns his back to you to speak rapidly to one of his crew.

Meanwhile the Doradan forces are busy arranging the transport of their prisoners—your ranger force—back to the Doradan territory. They move off, paying little attention to you because they trust Haven and his crew.

Haven seems engrossed in his conversation. Scanning the immediate area you see a metal rod about five feet long lying on the ground.

You think there's a chance for escape, if you can knock Haven out, get his weapon, and head for cover in the pinon trees.

You wait and watch. Haven concludes his talk, dismisses the crew members, and turns back to you. The two of you are now alone. The Doradans are out of sight.

If you decide to knock out Haven, turn to page 20.

If you decide not to use force, turn to page 77.

"We'll need all the help we can get," you say. "Those Doradans never give up."

You look at Marileva. She nods in agreement.

"Please ask for permission to lead a preemptive strike on the Doradan capital," you go on. "An emergency session of Congress should give it to us."

Marileva nods again and uses her communicator, scrambling the message to avoid interception by any Doradan listening posts. Haven invites you and Marileva inside his spacecraft. During the two hours that you anxiously await the Turtalian Congress's okay you learn of Haven's home galaxy, which is on the rim of the Outer Seat of Time.

"Do you mean, Haven, that between here and there, with all those billions of planets and stars, only Earth seems like a suitable place for your people?"

Haven is still in his humanoid form. He grins and replies, "What seems like an impossible numbers of stars and planets to you is a mere trifle to us. But the answer is yes. Earth is a comfortable place for us. And it is one of the truly hopeful and bright spots in the universe."

"That is, if you do not destroy yourselves in the way our planet is busy doing," he adds, looking grim.

Turn to page 23.

"You'd better be for real, Haven. Denver will blow us both out of the sky in a microsecond, if they suspect treachery." You don't feel secure about the decision, but it seems the best way to get out of the mess you're in.

Haven nods, and you enter his spacecraft. As the craft heads for Denver, you give Haven the proper security codes. Seconds before you arrive, he gives a command to his crew. The beam of azure light that earlier froze your action incapacitates you once again.

Denver base reads Haven's maneuvers as hostile. The Tactical Strike Command fires a circular barrage. You, Haven, and the spacecraft merge with the universe.

The End

"I believe Turtalians share your interests," you answer Jeremy. "The Corporation is as dangerous to us as the Doradans are. Now that the two are in league, we're all worse off. Yes, we'll give you direct help—personnel, equipment, supplies. First, though, what about Matt and Mimla? Where are they?"

Jeremy looks at you. He's not a friendly type, you think.

"If you came from Turtalia, then you flew over the area where they had a camp. They're trying to trace a Doradan assault team. Big things could be up. Doradans are all over the place. It looks like the buildup for an attack on the Turtalian western border."

"When did you last hear from them?" you demand.

"A week ago. Apparently they were attacked. They're still out there, I guess."

"How far from here?" you ask.

"Eighty, maybe a hundred miles," he responds. "It's quicker to fly, but there is also a road. We have some motorcycles. They're old, but they'll do."

If you decide to use the road to search for Matt and Mimla, turn to page 80.

If you decide to fly to the camp, turn to page 71.

"You're asking for too much," you say to Jeremy. "But I will offer to lead a mission into Corporation territory to check out their strength, if you'll help me find Matt and Mimla."

Jeremy reluctantly accepts. That evening you and three of the Rebels slip across the bay by boat. Night makes San Francisco an eerie place. Here and there pinpricks of light glow from candles or lanterns. Electricity is found only in one small area at the top of Nob Hill.

Your scouting shows you that the Corporation forces are spread out and few in number. Perhaps most of them are out in the hills with the Doradans. Or perhaps the image of the fearsome Corporation is largely the result of a big publicity campaign.

Hours later you and the Rebels return to the Hungry Pelican with your report.

"I should have known," says Jeremy. "Phonies, they're all phonies. Well, you lived up to your bargain. We'll see what we can do about Matt and Mimla. They're out in the hills somewhere, that much we know. I'll take you there."

Jeremy is true to his word. He leads you to a friendly camp where Matt and Mimla are hiding out in the mountains east of the city. They've obtained vital intelligence about a planned Doradan attack. Now the only task left is to fly them home and warn Turtalia.

The End

"October 15, 1981," you answer.

"It was a great day," he replies and heads for the back of the restaurant. "Come with me."

Two men leave the counter and stand by the front door. You follow the waiter into a back room.

"Okay. You know the code. Now what do you want? Who are you?" Jeremy asks.

"I'm a Turtalian. I want information on Matt and Mimla, my agents. Are they safe? Where are they? When were they here last?"

"You ask a lot of questions for a stranger. If we help you, what do we get? Will Turtalia join us against the Corporation? We're desperate now."

If you decide to pledge to work against the Corporation, turn to page 68.

If you bargain with Jeremy, and avoid pledging direct Turtalian aid, turn to page 87.

"I'll fly," you say. "Get me someone who knows the area."

Jeremy nods, and returns to the restaurant counter. Moments later a woman of about fifty enters the back room. She's quite thin, but the lines around her face make you think that she was fat at one time. These are hard times, and food is scarce.

The woman stares at you. Her suspicion and hostility are obvious. You sense that no one here feels anyone can be trusted.

"So, you want to know where those two are, is that it?" she asks rather nastily.

"That's right. Will you show me on this map?" you reply, pushing one of your flight maps to her.

She takes it and scans it with intensity, her finger poised over the surface.

Turn to page 84.

"I'm sure the Turtalian Congress will appreciate your kind offer, Haven," you reply. "But time is of the essence, and I do have a ranger strike force that can be utilized. Perhaps a strike at their main operations base will nip this in the bud."

"As you wish, Commander, but you Earthlings do seem to make things confusing. Let's hope you are right. I will watch. If you need help, call."

Haven dematerializes.

"I hope he's gone back inside his spacecraft," you say to Marileva. "We'd better get moving, too. Do you have any ideas on how to proceed?"

"Why don't you and I slip into Dorado, head for the operations base, and knock it out ourselves?" she suggests. "No fuss, no mess."

You appraise the situation carefully. Two people in civilian clothes could go virtually unnoticed; a larger strike force of uniformed rangers would not.

If you go into Dorado with Marileva, turn to page 78.

If you decide to use the whole ranger strike force, turn to page 82.

As you bounce along, you're sorry you chose the motorcycles over the plane. The highways and roads haven't been cared for in years, and they're a mass of potholes and weeds.

The bikers seem oblivious to it all. They merrily roar on at high speed, rocketing over the bumps and vegetation.

"How far did you say it was?" you yell at your driver. He doesn't answer.

"How far?" you yell again.

He just grins and accelerates. The old Harley belches smoke and keeps roaring.

Turn to page 79.

You're led over hilly, grassy terrain for nearly an hour. The initial excitement of the landing and of being captured wears off and fatigue sets in. After all, you flew your motor-glider for over eight hours with no rest. You wish you'd finally get to wherever you're being taken.

Ten minutes later, your wish is fulfilled. You enter a camp that consists of a motley collection of tents, relics of happier times when hiking and climbing were weekend or vacation sports in California. The fabric of the tents—faded orange, yellow, tan—is worn, but they do provide shelter.

"Sit," Sellers urges you. "What do you drink? Coffee? Tea? Not that it matters. We only have herb tea, made from stuff we find along the way."

He sits down next to you, and commands, "Tell your story."

Turn to page 85.

"Well, a thing like this can't be decided immediately," you say to Haven. "Let me talk with my people. I can't take individual responsibility for this type of decision. Who'd believe me, anyway?"

Haven shakes his head in what looks like resignation and despair.

"So few have faith. You are not trusting your instincts. Or perhaps you are. You think this is all a Doradan hoax. I can see it in your face. Well, maybe I am wrong. Perhaps Turtalia is not for us. You are stalling, and time is precious for us now. I have wasted years on Earth already. We need help, and we need it now. You do not believe me. You do not trust me!"

Turn to page 39.

"Force begets force," you tell yourself, quoting one of the sayings of the Turtalian Congress. "I'd better wait and see what happens."

You fiddle some more with the communicator. You haven't fooled Haven. He takes the communicator from you and puts it in his pocket.

"I will not force you to contact your base, Commander, but it is a shame that we cannot cooperate. There is much to be lost if we do not. I have a plan. Perhaps it will prove to you the seriousness of my interest in working with the Turtalian people."

You nod your head, more out of habit than in agreement with what he's just said.

"My plan is this: I will tell the Doradan commander that I am taking you back to Dorado for questioning. In reality, we will go to the Turtalian capital, Denver. I cannot keep up this charade of being a Doradan agent any longer. What do you say?"

You ponder this. To bring Haven and his spacecraft to Denver using the special security codes could cause disaster to Turtalia if Haven turns out to be a fraud. He could launch a devastating strike on Turtalia.

If you decide to take Haven to Denver, turn to page 67.

If you decide to take Haven on a flight away from both Dorado and Denver, turn to page 105.

"Let's take care of this ourselves, Marileva," you say, agreeing to her idea.

Eleven hours later, you and Marileva are trapped in front of Doradan headquarters.

"We never had a chance," you say to Marileva in the few seconds you have left before the Doradans move in. "From the moment we stepped onto Doradan soil, we were doomed to failure because of the simplest of mistakes. When we changed into civilian clothes, we forgot to change our shoes. Turtalian military-issue shoes leave a distinctive tread pattern that even a child can spot."

Marileva has no time to respond and the Doradans ask no questions. A blast of automatic fire ends your promising careers.

The End

Three hours later you cross a high pass and begin to descend into a long valley of rolling, forested hills.

You wonder why you haven't been stopped by hostile Corporation or Doradan patrols. Then again, everything about this area is disorganized.

The goggles the bikers gave you are covered with dirt, and you have to keep wiping them in order to see. The exhaust fumes make you sick to your stomach.

"How much farther?" you ask again.

The driver points ahead.

"There," he says.

Sure enough, over the next hill you come to an armed Rebel camp. The Rebels welcome the bikers, who have brought messages from people in Berkeley along with a few needed supplies.

But Mimla and Matt are not there.

"Where are they?" you demand.

"They're up at the other camp with a man named Sellers," one of the men answers.

Turn to page 9.

80

"Motorcycles sound fine to me," you say to Jeremy. "Let's get going."

"Take it easy. We'll get there," responds a man who's been standing in the doorway watching. "It takes time to arrange things. Be cool, man, be cool."

Several cups of herb tea later, you hear the sound of motorcycle engines. Three old Harley-Davidson bikes appear. Their riders are dressed in the leather jackets of the Heaven's Fools, a motorcycle club. The men are bearded and tough-looking.

One of the bikes has a sidecar, a little one-wheeled passenger seat, attached. You hope it's not for you, but a biker points at it and says, "Hop in."

You comply. He hands you a pair of goggles and a helmet.

"Let's split!" another biker says.

Turn to page 73.

You are pleased to see that your ranger strike force is eager and ready to go. The effects of the tear gas have completely worn off. Equipment is checked and rechecked, and additional helicopters are called in.

It takes two hours to round up the helicopters necessary for the mission. In the meantime, you send out search teams to look for any members of the Doradan strike force who may still be in the area. None are found.

The tense, grim rangers talk little as they're airlifted deep within Doradan airspace. You're surprised that there are no Doradan air patrols. The Doradans are busy arranging their attack on Turtalia, and their transports and aircraft are tied up in those preparations.

On schedule, according to synchronized watches, your helicopter squadron drops out of the sky in the Doradan capital and lands near the operations building. You leap out the open helicopter door and with the others, dash for the main door. Bullets pierce the air.

Turn to page 54.

"Hands up! Don't move!" you command.

The three most important Doradans are here: the leaders of the Doradan army, air force, and intelligence services.

"This way! Move fast!" you order. The commander of the army lunges for his weapon, but Marileva stops him with a downward smash to his forearm.

You hurry your prisoners back through the corridor, down the stairs, and out into the street. Your ranger force has managed to hold off Doradan reinforcements, but their losses have been heavy. One of the helicopters has been destroyed.

You, Marileva, and your prisoners, along with several rangers, board one of the remaining 'copters. Moments later, you're on your way out of Dorado.

A squad of Turtalian planes meets you and escorts you triumphantly home with what you hope is the biggest catch ever—the three fascist chiefs.

"Good work," Marileva says, putting her hand on your shoulder. "Perhaps real peace is now possible."

The End

"There," the woman says. "That's where they're supposed to be. Cocky, those two, that's what they were! So sure of themselves. That's a good way to get killed. If you ask me, you're wasting your time. They've been food for the buzzards for days now, I'd say." She turns and leaves.

The area she pointed to on the map is right where you spotted the campfires. The problem remains—which camps are friendly?

Jeremy returns. "Got what you want, have you? Well, better leave then. You attract too much attention. Don't forget, Turtalia has promised us help."

You nod agreement and head back to your plane. There are more people in the streets now. They move quickly and furtively.

"I'll be glad to get out of here," you say to yourself.

Turn to page 104.

So you do. Sellers nods from time to time as he listens to your story, but says nothing until you've finished.

"Humph! Sounds reasonable. Don't know these Matt and Mimla people, but I've heard of them. I could help, if . . ."

"If what?" you ask.

"Slowly, my friend, slowly. There's a criminal gang called the Corporation in charge of what's left of San Francisco. We're Rebels—a group of freedom fighters. Several groups like us are fighting the Corporation, but we're scattered. Communication is hard. Let's make a trade, you and me, okay?"

Turn to page 90.

"The controls are useless," you shout, although there's no one to hear you.

You have no time to waste. You're only fifteen hundred feet above the ground, and the helicopter is losing altitude quickly. You wrestle with the seat belt release. Finally it clicks open, and you push your way through the Plexiglas door. The slipstream buffets you against the side of the helicopter. The salty taste of blood fills your mouth, the result of a nasty gash you get when you bump your head leaving the cabin.

Whop! Your parachute snaps open and stops your tumbling fall through the murky, gas-laden cloud. You slump in the harness, legs swinging to and fro like a puppet on a string.

Moments later you're in clear air, not more than two hundred feet above the ground. Your head clears, too, and you prepare to land. There's no one around!

Where are my people? you wonder. Captain Ricardo and the rangers should be there.

Turn to page 27.

"I'm not really empowered by my government to commit us to armed involvement here," you reply. "I'll see what I can do, though."

Jeremy slams his hand down on a wooden table top.

"No guts. We're fighting for our lives, and you talk like a lawyer. We don't need you or your kind. Beat it, and good riddance." He turns and leaves.

What next? you think.

"Hey, wait a minute," you call after him. "Don't be so hasty. Let's talk. Maybe we can work something out."

You hope Jeremy will be reasonable. He turns, comes back, and looks you in the eyes.

"That's what your friends Matt and Mimla said. And what did we get? Nothing but trouble. You want to prove to us that you and Turtalia will help? Then go to the Corporation and negotiate a truce. That is, if you have the guts."

If you decide to give it a try and negotiate for a truce with the Corporation, turn to page 106.

If you offer instead to lead a reconnaissance mission to survey Corporation territory, turn to page 69.

I must still be dreaming, you think as you open your eyes. Mimla is leaning over you. Matt stands beside her.

"Thank heavens you found us, Commander," Mimla says. "We've been desperate to get in touch with you. The radio equipment was smashed in our last fight with the Corporation. How are you?"

"What? How did you get here?" you blurt, wide awake now.

"I brought them to verify who you are," says Sellers. He stands behind Matt. "I decided to make sure you weren't on the wrong side, so I drugged you. I knew all along where Matt and Mimla were camped."

He gives you a smile that disappears quickly. "Now comes the hard part. We're surrounded by Doradan and Corporation troops. In this light it won't take them long to spot your plane and come looking for you. Then we're in the soup."

Turn to page 99.

"What kind of trade?" you ask, wary of this man but half-believing his story of fighting for freedom against the criminal gang running San Francisco.

"A simple trade. You fly me to several other Rebel bases. I know where they are, or where they should be. I'll get them to help find your people, but meanwhile I get to coordinate our actions against Corporation units in the area. Is it a deal?"

"If it isn't, what then?" you ask.

"We wait until you decide that you want to cooperate. We have time. That's all we have, as a matter of fact."

If you decide to take Sellers to other Rebel bases, turn to page 24.

If you decide to wait it out, turn to page 11.

"Now!" you say to yourself.

Grabbing the rod, you jump to your feet. With a sweeping movement, you swing the rod toward Haven.

The metal rod clangs against an impenetrable and invisible barrier and bounces back. You're knocked off your feet by the force of the rebound, landing on your back.

Turn to page 109.

92

You start to feel you can't run anymore, at least not at the pace you've set. Your lungs feel as though they're about to burst. No one seems to have noticed you. Maybe you've slipped past all the attackers.

Hunkering down on the ground beside rocks and low bushes, you catch your breath and look back at the inferno you've just fled. The flashpoints of gunfire seem harmless from this distance. The only sound is a mild popping.

"I can't rest for long," you say to yourself and start off again. You walk at a fast pace, following the natural contour of the hills.

Hours pass. You nibble on a mint cake and raisin bar from your kit bag for energy. Dawn rapidly approaches. You feel you're free of the danger zone, at least for now.

Turn to page 96.

"I'll handle Mimla and Matt," you say to the red-faced lieutenant. "Get Captain Von Moschicker over here right away. She'll take care of Haven and the files. He's a fool to think he can escape."

"Yes, Commander," the lieutenant replies. She and the other officer exit your office.

Moments later, Captain Von Moschicker snaps you a smart salute. She stands at attention waiting for your instructions. You tell her about Haven's escape and the missing files.

"Captain, take any personnel you need," you order, "but get Haven and those files. I have faith in you. Remember, time is of the essence. Go to it, and good luck."

"Yes, Commander. We'll do our best."

"It will have to be more than your best. You must recover the files," you reply.

As the captain leaves, your lieutenant enters.

"Have we got a fix yet on where that message from Matt and Mimla came from?" you demand.

"Yes, Commander. One hundred miles east of San Francisco. The transmission was cut off before they completed the message, as you suspected."

"Okay. Get the new motor-glider ready. I'm going after them."

"By yourself, Commander?"

Turn to page 16.

Tension mounts as the day unfolds. You wait uneasily for darkness to fall. Enemy patrols are in the hills all around you. The tents in the Rebel camp have been dismantled and stowed away. Everyone stays under cover. No movement is allowed.

The Rebels lie with their weapons at the ready, scanning the horizon. Occasionally there are signs of activity far off in the distance. Your area seems to be immune to discovery or attack.

Finally night comes and it's time to leave for Turtalia. With good-byes and pledges of friendship, you, Matt, and Mimla quickly head toward the field where your plane is hidden.

The takeoff is dicey, but you make it and climb out of the valley. You bank and head due east. Your last look at the valley shows pinpricks of light from weapons fire. Corporation and Doradan troops are attacking the Rebel group.

Turn to page 102.

Physically, the part of Berkeley near the university seems pretty much unchanged. But many of the homes are abandoned, the people having fled to the country, afraid of the fighting among the three hostile groups.

You have a year-old map of the area provided by Turtalian intelligence. In the morning, you should be able to locate Jeremy at a restaurant called the Hungry Pelican.

You decide to spend the hours until daylight in one of the abandoned houses. Once inside, you sit down and pull out your map. Before you open it, the strain of your long flight overcomes you. Your eyes close.

Turn to page 98.

96

By the time daylight finally comes, you're in a pine forest on the slopes of steep hills that lead to mountains. You stop and pull a map out of your kit bag. The map indicates that you're near what was once a ski resort called Squaw Valley. It might be around the next mountain.

Then you hear a noise. It's the buzzing sound of a light plane, probably an observation plane. *Is it searching for me?* you wonder.

If you take cover and wait until the plane leaves, turn to page 118.

If you decide to go on, trying to stay hidden in the trees, turn to page 107.

When you wake up it's morning. The fog across the bay is beginning to lift. It's a beautiful day, but you feel lonely and sad as you walk along the empty, quiet streets.

The Hungry Pelican is open for breakfast, and twelve or fifteen people are huddled over a counter. When you enter, the babble of voices ceases. Slowly faces turn to look at you. You nod a greeting, yet the silence remains unbroken.

If you decide to take a seat at the counter, turn to page 58.

If you decide to back out and wait for a better time, turn to page 103.

Matt and Mimla confirm Sellers' report.

"What are our choices?" you ask.

Sellers crouches at the tent flap and looks at the first rays of dawn over the distant mountains. "We could try to hide the plane, cover it with brush, and hope they don't spot it. Or you three could try to make it to the plane and take off. Chances are those Doradans are still asleep; they're a lazy bunch."

If you decide to try to hide the plane and wait until night before taking off, turn to page 12.

If you decide to take off immediately, turn to page 113.

You talk fast, explaining that you're a Turtalian emissary who is also representing the Rebels.

The guard grunts and leads you into the hotel and across the lobby to the elevators. He gets on with you and punches the button for the twenty-first floor. When the doors slide open, he shoves you ahead of him into a suite of rooms.

There you see a man in his thirties with a beard and long hair, weaning dark glasses, a Hawaiian shirt, an earring, and silver bracelets. He grins at you and speaks.

"Come on in. Sit down. Want something to drink? No? Well, as you wish."

Turn to page 25.

"I hope the Rebels make it," Mimla says.

You nod grimly and turn back to watch your plane's course. Silently you add your own hope that you and your agents will make it. There's not much time left before the Doradan invasion spreads eastward. You push the motor-glider to top speed, racing the clock to get Matt and Mimla's vital intelligence back to Turtalia.

The End

Someone coughs, and most of the faces turn toward that person. "Here I go," you say to yourself as you back out the door, waving a weak goodbye to those at the counter still looking in your direction.

Whew! That smelled like trouble, you think.

Before you have a chance to get more than five steps away from the Hungry Pelican, a squad of thugs surrounds you.

"Looks like a spy to me—a perfect hostage," says the leader of the squad. "Take him away!"

Nylon rope is bound around your wrists, a gag is thrust in your mouth, and you're dragged away. No one comes to your aid. It's life as usual in this part of the country. True anarchy reigns. What's worse, it's said that most hostages out here don't live to tell their tale!

The End

104

Later that morning, you're safely airborne and heading east when you pick up a radio signal. You fiddle with your dial until the signal clears.

"Two licorice pizzas to go. Repeat, two licorice pizzas to go."

Matt and Mimla's code call!

You respond with a six-digit identifying number: "Zero, four, two, eight, one, seven."

"We read you. Pizza is ready for takeout," comes the response, followed by the coded coordinates of Mimla and Matt's position.

You fly to their campsite. Now it's a matter of landing safely, taking off quickly, and avoiding Doradans on the trip home. Matt and Mimla fill you in on the information they've collected.

"That's good stuff," you tell them. "I have no doubt it will help foil the Doradan attack."

The End

The security clearance codes and the coordinates you provide Haven lead you on a flight that ends over California.

Haven is not stupid and says, "Well, Commander, two can play this game."

The spacecraft leaps to hyperspace speed. You're rushed to the outer rim of the Wall of Stars, where you're interrogated by the Crystal People and used as a bargaining chip—a hostage—as they try to get what they need from Turtalia.

Good luck! Turtalia has a policy never to negotiate for hostages. You've always agreed with the policy. Now you aren't so sure.

The End

"Okay. I get your message," you say. "I'll see what I can do about negotiating a truce with the Corporation; you see what you can find out about Matt and Mimla. Deal?"

Jeremy grabs your hand and pumps it vigorously.

"Now, that's talking," he says.

You two spend the rest of the day planning your approach to the Corporation. Corporation headquarters is in an old hotel on top of Nob Hill.

Turn to page 110.

"I can't waste any more time," you say to yourself.

Keeping in the shadow of trees, you continue walking, hoping to escape the notice of the plane.

You wander through the Sierras for two days. At dawn of the second day, you're stopped by a Rebel patrol. They bring you into headquarters, a ski patrol shack in Squaw Valley. There you explain your mission and describe the attack on Sellers and his Rebels.

Then you get the bad news. "Your agents Matt and Mimla have been captured by Doradans," the Rebel commander tells you. "They're probably dead. You must stay with us. We're as vulnerable as Sellers and his Rebels. We're preparing for an attack. I'm sure you can help."

The loss of your agents saddens you deeply. You must inform Operations Center as soon as possible. For now, you know you must do as the commander says: stay with the Rebels and lend your talents to their effort to stop the Doradans. It will be the first of many battles to save Turtalia.

The End

"Oh, no!" you yell. "Those are alien ships, not Doradan planes!"

Desperately you attempt to dive away from the frightening fire coming from the strange craft hovering near you.

With a speed unknown to you, one of the crafts disappears. The other two converge on you.

"Help! Help, someone—anyone! They're going to get—"

Those are the last words you ever say.

The End

Haven peers down at you.

"I do not blame you, Commander. After all, why should you trust me? Talk is cheap, as you Earth types say. I fear, though, that we have to start trusting each other sometime. Let me help you aboard the spacecraft so we can talk some more. If I give you back the top-secret files you came after, maybe you will trust me."

There's nothing to do now but go with Haven. You aren't sure whether you're a prisoner or not, but at the moment, the choices are in the hands of this being called Haven.

You will need to do whatever it takes: talk, negotiate, plan. For now, survival is your main goal. You can only hope Haven is the forgiving type and will allow you to take back your earlier decision.

The End

110

The next morning you leave on a mission that fills you with fear. You travel from Berkeley to San Francisco by boat. The weather is foggy and damp. The trip across the bay is long and unpleasant. You're careful to avoid Corporation patrols.

Walking through San Francisco is like moving through a nightmare. The skyscrapers are silent, many of them burned out. Windows are smashed. Rusting cars line the roads. Some of them have been burned, too.

You barely escape getting caught by a patrol. But at last you make it up the long hill to the old hotel. It's a relic of the past—beautiful, elegant, and well-maintained in the midst of the destruction.

Fear paralyzes you as you walk up to the elaborately decorated front door.

"What do you want?" yells a voice.

Turn to page 101.

"It's now or never," you say. "Waiting here is just asking for it."

You, Matt, and Mimla head out toward the field where the Rebels have hidden your plane.

Just as you approach the field, a barrage of mortar and small-arms fire destroys the plane—and with it the hope for escape. Soon you will either be prisoners or dead. Time is all you have left, and you don't have much of that.

The End

Before Haven can reply, Marileva interrupts.

"The Turtalian Congress has replied in the affirmative," she announces, switching off her communicator. "The preemptive strike should be launched as soon as possible."

"Leave it to me," Haven replies.

He gives commands to his crew to guide the spacecraft to the Doradan capital. "We will stop the threat without harming anyone. Then it is up to you to change what is going on in Dorado. We could be a good team, you Earthlings and we Crystal People. As I said before, we need your help, too. We will talk about that later."

"I have a feeling you're right, Haven," you agree.

"By the way," he adds, "here are your top-secret files. We have no need of them. I took them only so that I could lure you to me."

The End

Once again, curiosity overcomes you. You agree.

The humanoid form next to Haven places a clear, glass-like bell over your head. Lights snap on and off. Your head fills with the glorious and awful history of a planet and civilization far off in a different galaxy. You begin to grasp the origin of the Crystal People. You become a part of their life force.

You no longer have any doubts about these creatures. Now you must try to convince others in Turtalia that the Crystal People need help. It won't be easy, but with the knowledge you've just gained, you're confident you'll succeed.

The End

118

The annoying buzzing sound gets closer and closer. The plane comes into view above the pine trees. It's an ultralight, a relic of the 1980s, when people flew the ridiculous planes for sport. Its main advantage today is that not much fuel is needed to operate it. Fuel is precious, particularly in the untamed lands of the west, which have been ravaged by fighting for years.

The ultralight zooms back and forth like a dragonfly. "What is it looking for?" you ask yourself aloud.

You realize that it's probably looking for you. But is it friend or foe? Maybe Sellers got a message out to other Rebels. Maybe they're trying to help. Maybe it's even Matt and Mimla, safe and searching for you!

Just as you decide to signal the plane, it turns. The sound of the engine recedes and then is gone. You stare at the sky for a long moment, then return to the task at hand: getting out of this wilderness, finding Matt and Mimla, and getting back to Turtalia.

Without your plane it's a tall order—almost impossible—but you decide not to think that way. Only relentless determination can conquer the impossible, you tell yourself as you trudge day after weary day.

On you go.

The End

CREDITS

This book was brought to life by a great group of people. R. A. Montgomery thought long and hard about how his adventures could be restored for today's reader, and brought this manuscript into the Internet age. Just down the hall, Shannon Gilligan took on the complex role of Publisher. Gordon Troy performed the legal pirouettes that result in proper trademark and copyright protections. Stacey Hood at Big Eyedea Visual Design in Swan Valley, Montana, was responsible for layout and design. Melissa Bounty offered editorial harmony wherever possible. Dale Schaft gracefully commanded Operations, and Jason Geller took control of National Sales. Adrienne Cady came onboard as Publisher's Assistant. Risa Rae and Robin Hagerman checked and rechecked all the numbers in Accounting. Dot Green and Peter Bowering gave these books a great digital home at www.cyoa.com. Finally, Sundance Publishing brought this story into classrooms across the United States.

Illustrator: Jason Millet. Since graduating from Chicago's American Academy of Art, Jason Millet has created artwork for companies ranging from Disney® to Absolut®. His client list includes Warner Brothers®, Major League Baseball®, the Chicago Bulls® and Hallmark®, among many others.

Cover Artist: Sittisan Sundaravej (Quan). Sittisan is a resident of Bangkok, Thailand and an old fan of *Choose Your Own Adventure*. He attended The University of the Arts in Philadelphia, where he received his BSC in architecture and a BFA in animation. He has been a 2D and 3D animation director for productions in Asia and the United States and is a freelance illustrator.

Cover Artist: Kriangsak Thongmoon (Tao). Kriangsak is a graphic artist living in Thailand. After attending Srinakarinwiroj Prasarnmitr University in Bangkok, Kriangsak made a career illustrating for various well-known publications in Thailand before switching his concentrations to 3D modeling and computer animation. However, his love for drawing and sketching still keeps him coming back to non-computer generated illustrations.

ABOUT THE AUTHOR

R. A. MONTGOMERY has hiked in the Himalayas, climbed mountains in Europe, scuba-dived in Central America, and worked in Africa. He lives in France in the winter, travels frequently to Asia, and calls Vermont home. Montgomery graduated from Williams College and attended graduate school at Yale University and NYU. His interests include macro-economics, geo-politics, mythology, history, mystery novels, and music. He has two grown sons, a daughter-in-law, and two granddaughters. His wife, Shannon Gilligan, is an author and noted interactive game designer. Montgomery feels that the new generation of people under 15 is the most important asset in our world.

For games, activities and other fun stuff, or to write to R. A. Montgomery, visit us online at CYOA.com

ADVENTURER'S LOG

ADVENTURER'S LOG

ADVENTURER'S LOG

ADVENTURER'S LOG

ADVENTURER'S LOG

ADVENTURER'S LOG

10.10.07

Are You Ready?

Beyond Escape Trivia Quiz

You've succeeded through a world of danger and mystery! But how many of THESE adventures did you take?

1) What is the capital of Turtalia?
A. Denver
B. Los Angeles
C. New York
D. Washington, D.C.

2) Who are two of your best agents, that you sent into land west of Turtalia?
A. Jack and Jill
B. Amy and Josh
C. Brian and Patricia
D. Mimla and Matt

3) Who was the Doradan spy who escaped?
A. Matt
B. Haven
C. Refuge
D. Harry

4) What is missing along with the spy?
A. Your favorite shoes
B. A computer
C. Three top-secret files
D. A pony

5) Who do you send to search for Haven?
A. Mimla
B. Captain Von Moshicker
C. Colonel Van Bruen
D. Captain Scoopy

6) What do you use for transportation?
A. Scooters
B. Hang gliders
C. Boats
D. Motor gliders

7) Who is the chief political officer of Turtalia?
A. Mimla
B. Matt
C. Haven
D. Marileva

8) What surprising fact about Haven do you discover?
A. He is actually 100 years old
B. He owns a chain of seafood restaurants.
C. He is actually not a human and also not a Doradan spy
D. His favorite food is Brussels sprouts

9) What is the name of the man who you are told is holding Matt and Mimla?
A. Buyers
B. Sellers
C. Tom
D. Gary

10) What crucial item do you run out of while fighting rebels with Sellers?
A. Guns
B. Whipped topping
C. Soap
D. Ammunition

Original Fans Love Reading
Choose Your Own Adventure®!

The books let readers remix their own stories—and face the consequences. Kids race to discover lost civilizations, navigate black holes, and go in search of the Yeti, revamped for the 21st century!
Wired Magazine

I love CYOA—I missed CYOA! I've been keeping my fingers as bookmarks on pages 45, 16, 32, and 9 all these years, just to keep my options open.
Madeline, 20

Reading a CYOA book was more like playing a video game on my treasured Nintendo® system. I'm pretty sure the multiple plot twists of *The Lost Jewels of Nabooti* are forever stored in some part of my brain.
The Fort Worth Star Telegram

How I miss you, CYOA! I only have a small shelf left after my mom threw a bunch of you away in a yard sale—she never did understand.
Travis Rex, 26

I LOVE CYOA BOOKS! I have read them since I was a small child. I am so glad to hear they are going back into print! You have just made me the happiest person in the world!
Carey Walker, 27